For Mike Pogue, a friend—B.G.

To Jasper—S.G.

Copyright © 1992 Rabbit Ears Productions, Inc., Rowayton, Connecticut.
Rabbit Ears Books is an imprint of Rabbit Ears Productions, Inc.
Published by Picture Book Studio, Saxonville, Massachusetts.
Distributed in the United States by Simon & Schuster, New York, New York.
Distributed in Canada by Vanwell Publishing, St. Catharines, Ontario.
Printed in Hong Kong.
1 2 3 4 5 6 7 8 9 10

Library of Congress Cataloging-in-Publication Data
Gleeson, Brian.
Anansi / written by Brian Gleeson ; illustrated by Steven Guarnaccia.
p. cm. — (We all have tales)
Summary: Two Jamaican folk tales in which Anansi the spider practices his trickery
on others. Includes an audio cassette featuring narration and music.
ISBN 0-88708-230-0. — ISBN 0-88708-231-9 (W/cassette)
1. Anansi (Legendary character)—Juvenile literature. 2. Tales—Jamaica.
[1. Anansi (Legendary character) 2. Folklore—Jamaica.] I. Guarnaccia, Steven, ill.
II. Title. III. Series.
PZ8.1.G4594An   1991
398.24'52544—dc20
[E]   91-40671
CIP
AC

Written by
Brian Gleeson

ANANSI

Rabbit Ears Books

Illustrated by Steven Guarnaccia

A long, long time ago, there was nothing in this world. Then there were fishes in the sea, then there were animals in the bush. And in the beginning there was one place. Africa was that place. Then there were people. And those people, in the beginning—when this world was new—they told stories. Africa stories. ◆ They told stories about the things they saw. They told stories about things they thought. They told stories about things they dreamt. ♟ Yah, mahn. Those people told stories all the time. ◆ Then one day a terrible thing happened. Many, many of those people were taken away from their homes in Africa. ◆ Men made them slaves. Men brought them in ships and took them to Jamaica to work. A sad, sad thing. Yah, mahn. ♟ They worked hard in Jamaica on the sugar plantations. It was tough going there. But they remembered the old stories. You see, they brought the old stories with them. ◆ The people in Jamaica still tell those stories. They tell about Anansi the Spider.

ow, Anansi, he is teeny-teeny, but he is smart. How else could he get all stories named for him? You see, Anansi owns all stories. When your mother tells you a story, or your grandfather tells you a story, they borrow Anansi's story. All stories belong to Anansi.

Now, stories didn't always belong to Anansi. In the beginning, all stories were Tiger's stories. Tiger owned all stories because he was the biggest and strongest animal in the bush. Tiger, he owned everything in the bush. Anansi, the tiniest in the bush, he owned nothing. When he whispered, no one heard. And when he hollered, the others in the bush they all just laughed at him. One day Anansi decided to go ask for something to be named for him. So Anansi went to the home of Tiger.

When he came to Tiger, Anansi bowed so low that his forehead touched the ground. He said, "Everything is named for you, Tiger. How come nothing is named for me? We give your name to everything: Tiger lilies, Tiger moths, Tiger stories, Tiger this and Tiger that. But nothing bears my name." "That is true," Tiger said. "You want something named for you? Is that what you say?" "Yah, mahn," Anansi said. "What do you want?" Tiger said. "I want all stories to be named for me," Anansi said. So Tiger, he thought to himself. "I will trick this boy. I will make a joke on Anansi!" "That's cool," Tiger said. "That's cool, mahn. I will name all stories for you, Anansi. But first, there's a little thing I ask for," Tiger said.

"Bring to me Snake, the one who lives by the river. Bring him to me alive on Saturday. Then you will have the stories."

ow, all the animals in the bush, they all laughed because Tiger made a fool out of Anansi. Snake is big-big-big-big, and Anansi the Spider, he is teeny-teeny-teeny.

Kling-Kling Bird laughed a big belly-laugh. Frog, he laughed, too. And Monkey, he jumped backwards over and over, he laughed so hard. Anansi could never catch Snake. He is too small.

Anansi said, "That's the deal, mahn. I will bring you Snake Saturday. Then all stories will be named for me." So Anansi left for home. He heard laughter in the bush wherever he went. All of the creatures, big and small, just laughed at him. Tiger tricked Anansi bad.

best in the noose. 🖋 Then Anansi waited. And he waited. And Snake came slithering down through the bush and saw the berries. 🖋 "Those berries will be my dinner!" Snake said. 🖋 So Snake lay across the vine and ate the berries. Now, Anansi pulled hard on the noose, but Snake was too heavy. Anansi pulled and pulled and pulled, but it was no good. The calaban failed. Snake ate all the berries. Then Snake went home.

Now, this was Monday. On Tuesday Anansi got a big idea. He thought it was a marvelous idea. Anansi decided to build a calaban to catch Snake. So he took a strong-strong vine and made a noose. He hid the vine in the grass. He set some berries that Snake loved

On Wednesday Anansi got a big-big idea. "This one will work," Anansi said. "Today I will catch Snake!" So Anansi dug a deep-deep hole by the side of the road and put grease on the sides and bottom of the hole and made it nasty and slippery. On the bottom he put six bananas. Now, Snake loves bananas. Anansi thought, "Snake will go in the slippery hole for the bananas and he won't be able to get out because the sides are too slippery! This will do the trick, this will do the trick!" So Anansi hid in the bush beside the road to wait. And Snake came slithering down the road. He was hungry for dinner. Snake saw the bananas at the bottom of the hole. Now he knew that the sides were slippery because of the grease, so he wrapped his tail around the trunk of a tree. Then Snake reached down in the hole and got the bananas. When he was finished eating he pulled himself out of the hole with his tail! Then Snake just crawled away, his belly full with Anansi's bananas! Anansi didn't have any bananas; Anansi didn't have Snake.

On Thursday Anansi got big, big, big, biggest idea of them all. He decided to make a fly-up and catch Snake. 🎩 "Yah, mahn, the fly-up will catch Snake," Anansi said. "The fly-up will catch Snake. Snake will put his head in the trap and it will go up! This will catch him good!" 🎩 So Anansi built the fly-up. And inside the trap Anansi put one egg for bait. Oh, Snake felt very happy when he saw the egg. He just lifted his head and stood up. Then he bent over and snatched the egg very easily, right out of the trap. He didn't even touch the trap! Not even the fly-up could catch Snake! 🎩 Friday morning came and Anansi was worried. Snake had taken all of Anansi's food. And Anansi hadn't caught Snake yet. 🎩 "Rotten luck," Anansi said. 🎩 So Anansi thought all day Friday. He sat on a pebble and thought hard how he could catch Snake. But nothing came to him. Anansi was going to lose

the deal with Tiger! 🎩 Then Saturday morning came. And this was the day that Tiger wanted to have Snake so that all stories could be named for Anansi. But Anansi had no way to catch Snake. This looked bad for Anansi. Yah, mahn. 🎩 Anansi felt like taking a walk down by the river. He went there and he thought. Then he came to Snake's hole. Snake was watching the sun come up. Snake's head was out of the hole, but his body was in the hole.

"Anansi, I'm very angry with you, mahn," Snake said. "All week you tried to catch me. First the calaban, then the slippery hole, and yesterday the fly-up. I have a good mind to eat you up," Snake said. "Yes, but I was just trying to prove that you are the longest thing in the world," Anansi said. "But everybody knows I'm the longest thing in the world," Snake said. Now Anansi had a plan. He just kept on talking, telling his own stories. "Snake," Anansi said, "are you longer than that bamboo tree over there? I think not!" Now, Snake had a lot of pride and he said, "I'm bigger than the biggest bamboo!" So, Anansi went and chopped down the bamboo tree with his teeny-teeny machete. He put it near Snake's hole. "I don't think so, Snake," Anansi said. "Why don't you come out of that hole and see for yourself?" Now, Snake knew he was long.

He moved quickly to prove it to Anansi. Snake lay down on top of the bamboo. "No, I don't think so," Anansi said. "Bamboo is longer. Look at it, Snake." And Snake saw that the bamboo was a little longer because his tail curled up at the end so it looked like bamboo was longer. "Tie my tail to the bamboo, Anansi. It's curled at the end. It needs to be straight. Tie it tight." So Anansi did what Snake said. He tied Snake's tail to the bamboo.

Now, Kling-Kling Bird saw what was going on and he called the other animals to watch. Frog came. Monkey came. Even Tiger came. ✒ "Just proving my point," Anansi said to the animals. He gave a wink to them all.

✒ "Snake, you are long, but you are curled up even at your belly," Anansi said. ✒ "Then tie me there, too. And tie it tight. I will show you I'm longer than the bamboo!" ✒ So Anansi did what Snake said. He tied Snake's belly to the bamboo. The animals that were watching didn't make a peep. They couldn't believe what they were seeing. ✒ "Snake, you are still shorter than the bamboo," Anansi said. "Not much though, about six inches." ✒ "What should I do now?" Snake begged Anansi. ✒ "I think you can do it," Anansi said. "You have to stretch hard, mahn. You have to stretch so hard that your skin pulls up and your eyes close. Make yourself longer, mahn."

✒ "Stretch long, Snake!" all the animals said. "Stretch long!" ✒ And Snake stretched long. He kept stretching and the animals called to him, "You're winning, Snake, you're almost longer than the bamboo."

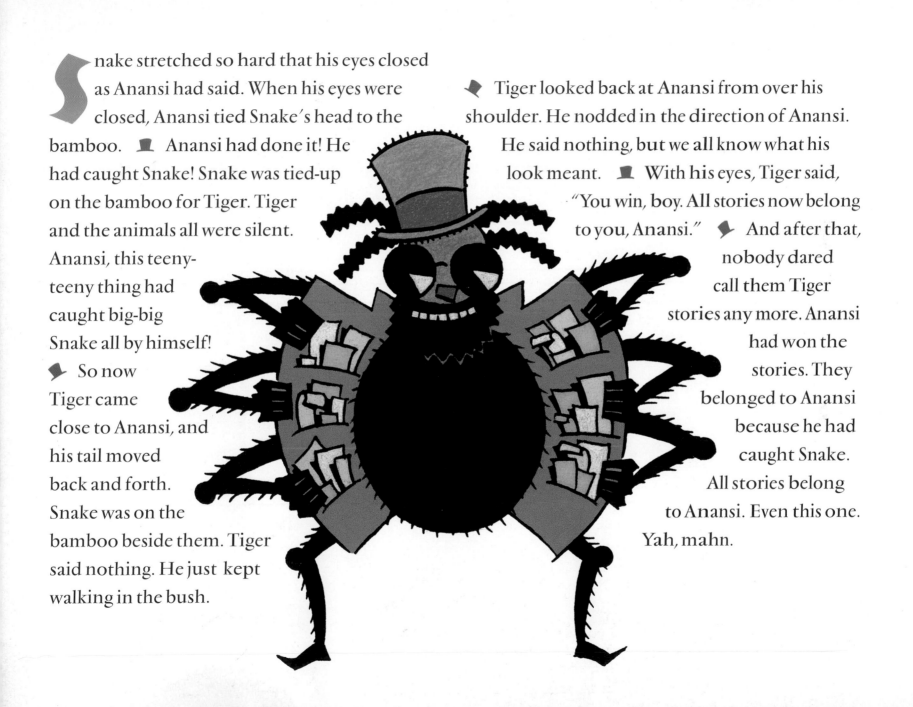

nake stretched so hard that his eyes closed as Anansi had said. When his eyes were closed, Anansi tied Snake's head to the bamboo.   Anansi had done it! He had caught Snake! Snake was tied-up on the bamboo for Tiger. Tiger and the animals all were silent. Anansi, this teeny-teeny thing had caught big-big Snake all by himself!

   So now Tiger came close to Anansi, and his tail moved back and forth. Snake was on the bamboo beside them. Tiger said nothing. He just kept walking in the bush.

   Tiger looked back at Anansi from over his shoulder. He nodded in the direction of Anansi. He said nothing, but we all know what his look meant.   With his eyes, Tiger said, "You win, boy. All stories now belong to you, Anansi."   And after that, nobody dared call them Tiger stories any more. Anansi had won the stories. They belonged to Anansi because he had caught Snake. All stories belong to Anansi. Even this one. Yah, mahn.

ow, one time a story got Anansi into trouble. This story was so big that it made Anansi the Spider bald! It's true, mahn. Look at Anansi now. He has no hair on his head. He's bald like a mango.  This is how it happened. Anansi's mother-in-law died. It was a sad time for his wife, so Anansi sent her to the funeral without him. Anansi said to his wife, "Go ahead, wife. I'll soon come to mother-in-law's funeral." Anansi had to think hard. He was a big-big man. He stayed at home to figure how he could be special at the funeral.

After his wife had gone he thought how he was going to show his big sadness at his mother-in-law's funeral. "Everyone will eat at the funeral. I will be different. I will not eat for seven days!" Anansi said. "This will show that I have the most sorrow of everyone at the funeral, make me a big-big man!" But first, before he went, he ate everything in his house. He ate for three hours. Mangos, plantains, yams—he ate everything. Anansi ate so much that he got a big stomach ache. His belly was full, mahn. Then Anansi went to his mother-in-law's funeral.

After Anansi's mother-in-law was buried the other animals said, "Eat Anansi, eat. You have a long trip. You must eat."  "What kind of man eats after his mother-in-law is buried?" Anansi said. "I don't eat to show my sorrow. I will eat on the eighth day." So Anansi didn't eat. The animals thought he must be sad. Nobody ever starved himself because his mother-in-law was buried. The animals thought he was a good man to show his respect. The second day came and Anansi ate nothing. All of the animals said, "Eat Anansi. You must eat!" "What kind of man eats after his mother-in-law is buried?" Anansi said. "I'll eat on the eighth day." Now, the other animals ate a feast, mahn. But Anansi just watched. He got prouder second by second. The third day came and Anansi ate nothing. The

animals said, "Eat Anansi. You don't need to starve." "What kind of man eats after his mother-in-law is buried?" Anansi said. "I will eat on the eighth day." But this got hard for Anansi. Three days is a long time to go without food. He was starving to death. His belly hurt, he was so hungry. He watched the other animals eat their meal. He watched Monkey eat rice and Anansi could taste it in his own mouth. Anansi was so hungry that he dreamed of food at night when he slept.

The fourth day came and Anansi's head was spinning around and around, he was so hungry. All the animals were still asleep, so Anansi went for a walk to take his mind off food. Anansi walked and he saw a pot of beans cooking on a fire that was very hot. He couldn't control himself. He went right for the beans. He was going to eat! There is no one here. For better or for worse, he was going to eat now. So, Anansi stuck the spoon in the pot and snatched the beans and stuffed them in his mouth. He ate fast-fast-fast-fast-fast, he was so hungry. Anansi stuck the spoon in the pot again. This time he thought better. He thought he would take the beans into the bush and eat them in peace and quiet, so that nobody would see him eating. But when he lifted the spoon out of the pot, he heard the other ones coming. Pig, Rabbit, Dog, Kling-Kling Bird, and Monkey came walking toward the beans—and Anansi! Anansi thought quick. He poured the hot-hot beans into his hat. Then Anansi put that hat with the hot beans on his head. The animals said, "Eat Anansi. You must eat." But Anansi still went along with his story. "What kind of man eats after his mother-in-law is buried? I'll eat on the eighth day."

But this time it was different. Those beans were burning his head bad, mahn. The heat was so strong that Anansi's eyes were popping out of his head. So Anansi took his hat and moved it forward and backward, side to side. But the heat got worse on Anansi's head! He jumped and shook about, getting real lively. He did this so much it was funny. 🎩 "What are you doing with your hat there, mahn?" said Dog. "Do you have a honeybee in there?" 🎩 But Anansi had another story to tell. 🎩 "Today is the day of the Hat-Shaking Dance in the village where I grew up," Anansi said. "It is a great dance. We do it like I do." 🎩 Anansi was shaking and dancing all over, just jiggling his hat all around. He couldn't stand still, the beans were so hot! He was burning up under his hat! 🎩 "I must go to my village and do the Hat-Shaking Dance with my people," Anansi said. "The festival is too much fun to miss! They need me there!" 🎩 So, Anansi pushed through all the animals, shaking and jiggling his hat. He moved very quickly to get out of there. Smoke was coming out of his hat, his head was burning so badly. 🎩 "But you must eat, Anansi," the animals said. "Before your journey you must eat." 🎩 "What kind of man eats after his mother-in-law is buried?" Anansi said.

nansi ran as quickly as a mongoose, but the animals were still behind him. They still begged him to eat. "Eat, Anansi," the animals said. "You must eat."

Now the hot beans were hurting Anansi's head badly. Anansi could only think about getting that hat off his head. He couldn't stand it anymore! So Anansi took off his hat and those hot-hot beans came tumbling down all over his head and face.

And all of the animals saw the beans dripping on Anansi's head. Pig saw it. Rabbit saw it. Dog saw it. Kling-Kling Bird saw it. And Monkey saw it. They stopped right there in their tracks. They knew Anansi was no big man. He said he wouldn't eat out of respect for his mother-in-law, but he had been eating all along! He was telling stories again.

"Such a big man!" Monkey said. "Oh no, no, no, I can't eat," said Kling-Kling Bird, in a mocking voice just like Anansi's. "What kind of man eats after his mother-in-law is buried?!"

Well, the animals all laughed at Anansi. They scorned him. And jeered him.

Anansi ran away from them. He was very ashamed that he had told a story and gotten caught. He ran into the bush and cleaned his head. And he rubbed all the beans off his head.

Now, when Anansi rubbed the beans from his head, he didn't feel any hair there anymore. Yah, mahn. The top of his head was shiny. Those beans burned his hair right off his head!  Now, this made Anansi be more ashamed. He went back to his home and thought some more. He sat in his web and thought a long, long time about his mistake. To this day, Anansi the Spider is still bald. Yah mahn. Bald like a mango. So, if you tell an Anansi story, tell the good story. Not the bad one. You don't want your head to be bald like Anansi if you tell the bad one. Tell the good Anansi story all the time. Yah, mahn:

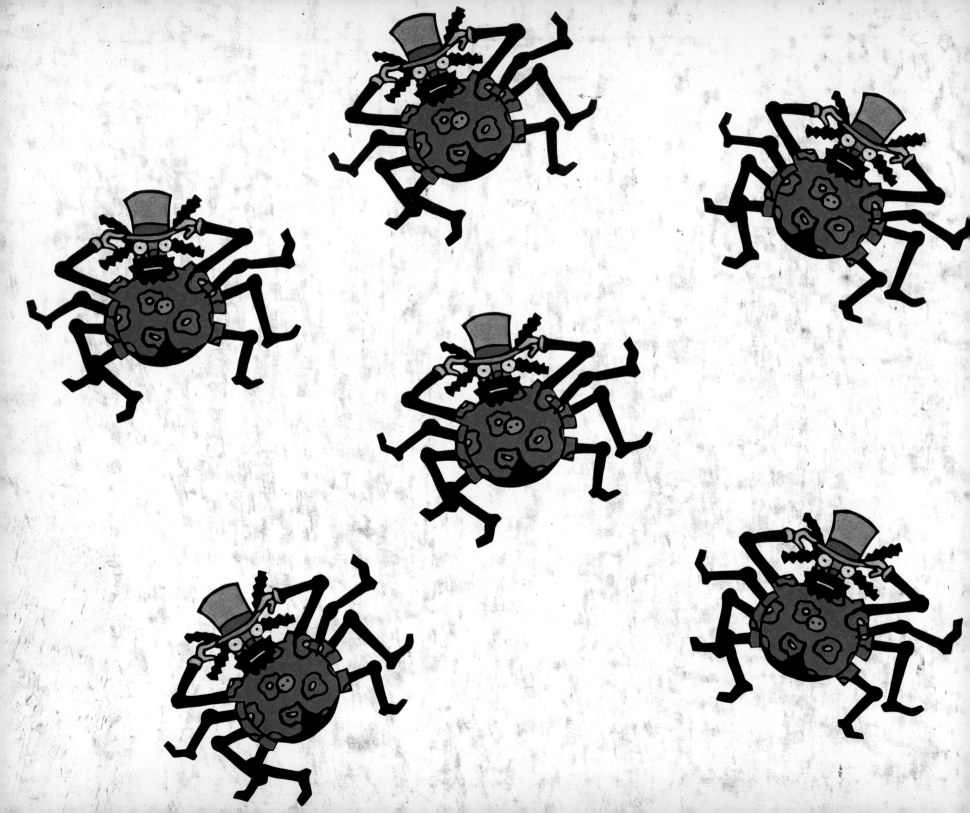